This book belongs to

_____

This book is dedicated to my children - Mikey, Kobe, and Jojo.
Keep asking questions and learning shall never cease.

Curious Ninja

By Mary Nhin

Pictures by
Jelena Stupar

I used to not be very interested in much...

And I was easily bored...

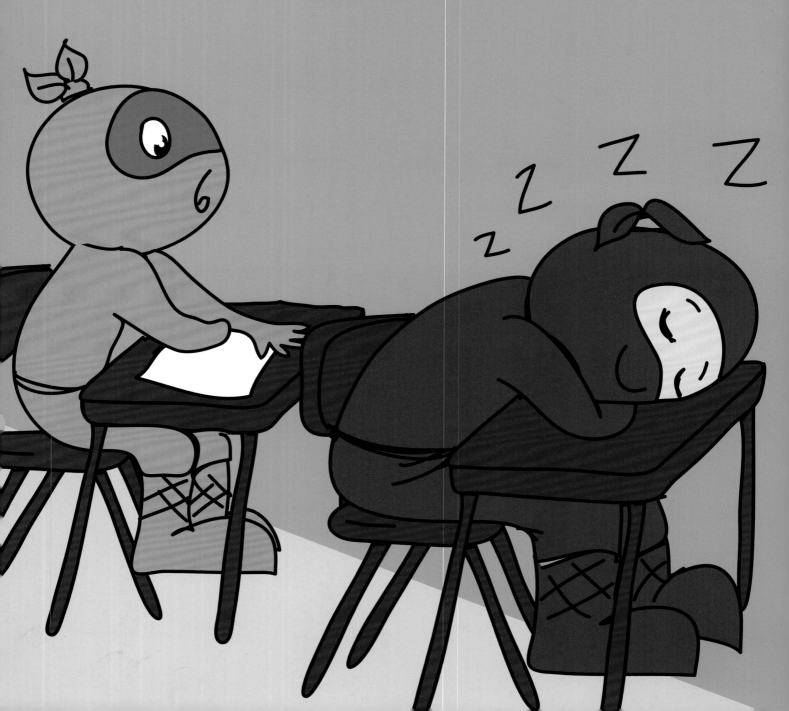

Sometimes, I would get negative...

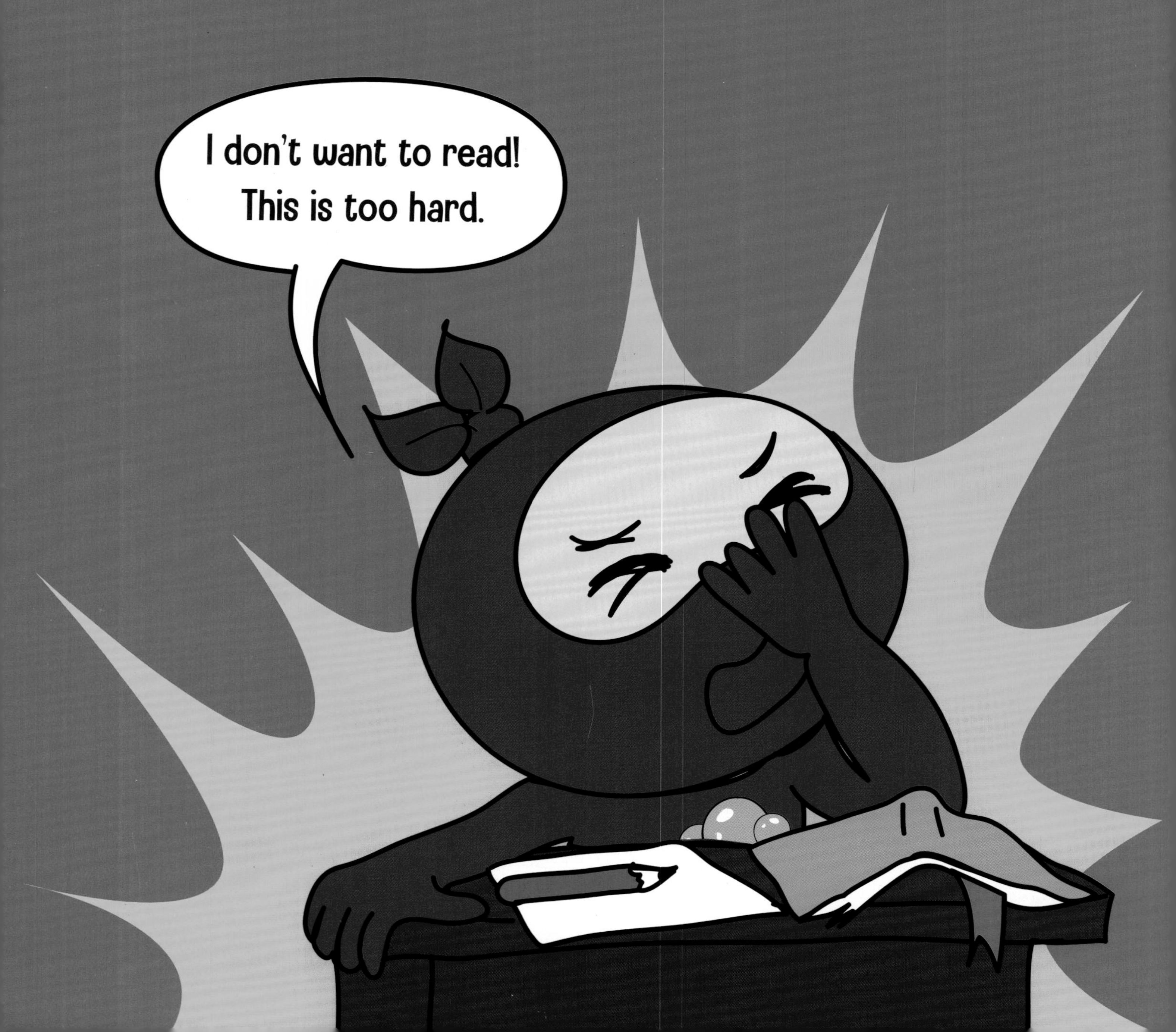

I began to wonder if I would ever become
interested in anything so I started walking...

I wandered the neighborhood in search of answers.

Ask questions.

It's great when we find out more information about things by **asking** questions. We can learn so much!

Be positive.

When we use positive thoughts and words, we choose to focus on what's good instead of what's negative.

Sometimes to grow we have to conquer our fears. This helps us develop curiosity and become a person of action, change, and success.

So I gave it a try...

I asked questions...

Why is this book called Charlotte's Webb?

I tried being positive...

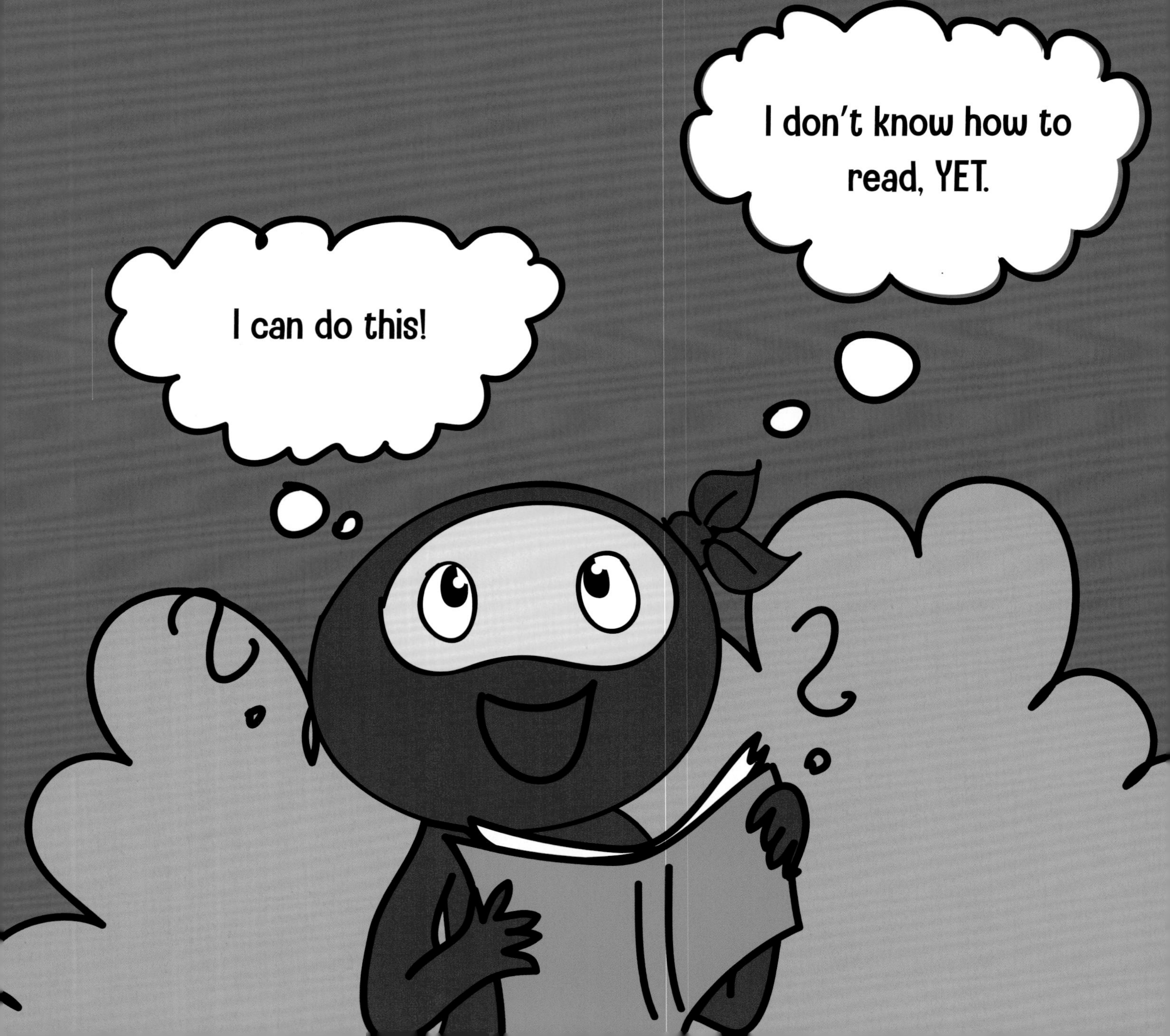

And I conquered my fears by trying to read...

Now, I'm Curious Ninja!

And I'm really good at ABC!

Remembering AB**C** could be your secret weapon
in developing your superpower - curiosity!!

Visit ninjalifehacks.tv for fun freebies!

@marynhin   @GrowGrit
#NinjaLifeHacks

Mary Nhin   Ninja Life Hacks

Ninja Life Hacks